Acting Edition

Pete the Cat

Book & Lyrics by
Sarah Hammond

Music by
Will Aronson

Based on the *New York Times* Bestselling *Pete the Cat*® Book Series by
Kimberly and James Dean

Originally Commissioned, Developed and Produced by
TheaterWorksUSA

Music Orchestrated and Produced by
Frank Galgano and Matt Castle

FOR PRODUCTION INQUIRIES

UNITED STATES AND CANADA
info@concordtheatricals.com
1-866-979-0447

UNITED KINGDOM AND EUROPE
licensing@concordtheatricals.co.uk
020-7054-7298

Each title is subject to availability from Concord Theatricals Corp., depending upon country of performance. Please be aware that *PETE THE CAT* may not be licensed by Concord Theatricals Corp. in your territory. Professional and amateur producers should contact the nearest Concord Theatricals Corp. office or licensing partner to verify availability.

No one shall make any changes in this title(s) for the purpose of production. No part of this book may be reproduced, stored in a retrieval system, scanned, uploaded, or transmitted in any form, by any means, now known or yet to be invented, including mechanical, electronic, digital, photocopying, recording, videotaping, or otherwise, without the prior written permission of the publisher. No one shall share this title(s), or any part of this title(s), through any social media or file hosting websites.

For all inquiries regarding motion picture, television, online/digital and other media rights, please contact Concord Theatricals Corp.

THIRD-PARTY MATERIALS USE NOTE

Licensees are solely responsible for obtaining formal written permission from copyright owners to use copyrighted third-party materials (e.g., incidental music not provided in connection with a performance license, artworks, logos) in the performance of this play and are strongly cautioned to do so. If no such permission is obtained by the licensee, then the licensee must use only original materials and materials that the licensee owns and controls. Licensees are solely responsible and liable for clearances of all third-party copyrighted materials, and shall indemnify the copyright owners of the play(s) and their licensing agent, Concord Theatricals Corp., against any costs, expenses, losses and liabilities arising from the use of such copyrighted third-party materials by licensees. For music, please contact the appropriate music licensing authority in your territory for the rights to any incidental music not provided in connection with a performance license.

IMPORTANT BILLING AND CREDIT REQUIREMENTS

If you have obtained performance rights to this title, please refer to your licensing agreement for important billing and credit requirements.

PETE THE CAT was first produced by TheaterWorksUSA in a tour of the New York City area that began on May 3, 2016. The performance was directed by Dan Knechtges, with assistant direction by Zi Alikhan, musical direction by James Dobinson, sets by Rob Odorisio, and costumes by Jennifer Caprio. The Production Stage Manager was Brendan O'Brien. The cast was as follows:

PETE THE CAT. . . . . .Travis Artz

JIMMY BIDDLE. . . . . Spencer Glass

OLIVE BIDDLE. . . . . Brandi Porter

MOM. . . . . .Samantha Owen

DAD . . . . Kevin Zak

PETE THE CAT received its Off-Broadway premiere, produced by TheaterWorksUSA, at the Lucille Lortel Theatre on July 25, 2017. The performance was directed by Dan Knechtges, with assistant direction by Zi Alikhan, musical direction by Miriam Daly, sets by Rob Odorisio, costumes by Jennifer Caprio, and orchestrations by Frank Galgano and Matt Castle. The Production Stage Manager was Phillip B. Richard II. The cast was as follows:

PETE THE CAT. . . . . .Kyle Sherman

JIMMY BIDDLE. . . . . .Adante Carter

OLIVE BIDDLE. . . . . Brandi Porter & Beth DeMichele

MOM . . . . Sam Tedaldi

DAD . . . . Matt Dengler

UNDERSTUDIES . . . . .Jodi Snyder & Ryan Edward Armstrong

CHARACTERS

PETE THE CAT – A super zen, rocking cat who lives in a VW Bus. He goes with the flow.

JIMMY BIDDLE – A very put-together second grader. He likes to prepare and tends to overthink things.

OLIVE BIDDLE – Jimmy's rambunctious sister. In Pre-K. She just loves everyone and everything.

MOM – Jimmy's nervous mom. Secretly, a rock star.

DAD – Jimmy's nervous dad. Secretly, a rock star.

Doubling:

MOM – **GRUMPY TOAD, MRS. CREECH,** the **MONA LISA.**

DAD – **GUS THE PLATYPUS, BARNABY** (a student), a **SHARK.**

OLIVE – **CAT-CATCHER, ELOISE** (a student), **ASTRONAUT.**

AUTHOR'S NOTES

A note on style

When Pete plays guitar, he makes guitar sounds with his mouth, like kids playing air guitar. Sometimes other people in the cast do, too. It's the way they rock out.

About the Bus

The Bus is a beloved friend and its honks should be treated by Jimmy and Pete as dialogue. In the original production, Pete's Bus was a two-dimensional moving set piece that Pete, Jimmy, and Olive sat inside of to "drive" around. They could move it side to side and forward and backward, but the sense of its whirlwind journey was mainly created by the work the whole ensemble did to change the world around the Bus as it went, as well as our heroes' reactions to each new destination.

SONG LIST

For Mom, Dad and Luke. – W.A.

For Owen and Maud, and also for Jam, the best of street cats. – S.H.

Scene One: Opening

[MUSIC NO. 01 – LIFE IS AN ADVENTURE]

(A backyard.)

*(**PETE** enters, rocking.)*

PETE. Yo diddleeoh! My name is Pete the Cat.

> *(**GUS THE PLATYPUS** and **GRUMPY TOAD** follow.)*

And this is my band! Grumpy Toad

> *(**GRUMPY** makes excited sound!)*

and Gus the Platypus.

> *(**GUS THE PLATYPUS** goes "eep.")*

We are here to welcome you to the backyard...or as I like to call it Animal Square Garden!

(They rock out.)

*(**JIMMY** sings from offstage.)*

PETE.

I PUT ON MY BEST RED BRAND NEW SHOES.
I GOT MY GUITAR AND A GROOVY BEAT.

**GRUMPY TOAD,
GUS & JIMMY.**

PETE.

	GROOVY BEAT.
I GOT THE BEST BAND OUT ON THE ROAD	OO...OO.
	THE JAM JAMMINEST.
MY NAME'S PETE!	
I MAKE A NEW FRIEND IN EV'RY TOWN.	OO...
BUT NOTHIN' CAN TIE ME DOWN.	AHH
ALL MY LIFE,	OO. HOO...
I HAVE LIVED BY ONE SIMPLE CODE:	OO. HOO...
	ONE SIMPLE CODE.
LIFE IS A REALLY, REALLY, REALLY BIG ADVENTURE.	AHH...
	BE NE NEOW!
A GROOVALICIOUS BEAUTIFUL ADVENTURE.	AHH...
	BE NE NEOW!
IT'S AWESOME TO BE ON A BIG ADVENTURE.	AHH... VENTURE!
THE OPEN AIR, I'M FANCY FREE,	BOP. BOP.
MY GROOVY BANDMATES AND ME.	BOP. BOP.

GRUMPY TOAD.

BLLEROW...

GUS THE PLATYPUS. Pete, should we be in this backyard?

PETE. Gus, don't ruin my jam.

GRUMPY TOAD. It's Pete. Every yard is Pete's yard.

GUS THE PLATYPUS. I just don't want the Cat-Catcher to catch Pete making noise after bedtime.

PETE. Nobody's caught me yet!

>*(They start jamming, call and response.* **PETE** *riffs like crazy.)*

BEO-NEO-NEOW NA NEO-NEOW...

BAND.

BEO-NEO-NEOW NA NEO-NEOW...

PETE.

BEO-NEO-NEOW NA NEO-NEOW...

BAND.

BEO-NEO-NEOW NA NEO-NEOW

PETE.

BLRREO-NEOW!

BAND.

BLRREO-NEOW!

PETE.

BE-NE-LE BE-NE-LE BE-NE-LE BE-NE-LE.

BAND.

BE-NE-LE BE-NE-LE BE-NE-LE BE-NE-LE.

>*(**PETE** gets carried away, riffing.)*

PETE. NEOW NEOW NA NA NA, NA NA OOO AHH OOO

>*(A very mean* **CAT-CATCHER** *shows up behind* **PETE** *as he jams. The* **BAND** *shuts up and tries to signal* **PETE** *to stop riffing. They say, "Pete Pete Pete Pete," but he doesn't notice, until...)*

PETE. Uh. Is the Cat-Catcher...right behind me?

CAT-CATCHER. *(Darkly.)* Pete the Cat.

GUS THE PLATYPUS. The Cat-Catcher!

PETE. Scram!

START TRACK 01B

> *(Sirens! The **BAND** scrambles. Crazy chase!)*

GUS THE PLATYPUS.	**GRUMPY TOAD.**
Holy moly!	Watch it! Whoa!

CAT-CATCHER. Catch that cat!

PETE. *(Caught. Rock-wail.)* Whoa-ow!

> *(**GUS** and **GRUMPY** watch sadly as the **CAT-CATCHER** catches **PETE** by the tail.)*

GUS THE PLATYPUS. *(Spoken in rhythm.)*
OH NO!

GRUMPY TOAD.
NOT PETE!

GUS THE PLATYPUS.
OH DEAR!

CAT-CATCHER. Pete the Cat, too much noise. Cats can't be out on the loose making this kind of racket.

PETE. Oh man.

CAT-CATCHER. Someone needs a very long time-out in a house. One week.

GRUMPY TOAD. One week! That's forever!

GUS THE PLATYPUS. *(Aside.)* But we're going to Paris – we're gonna jam!

GRUMPY TOAD. Without Pete?

GUS THE PLATYPUS. *(Agonized.)* They're gonna make Pete a housecat.

GRUMPY TOAD. I can't watch.

(The **CAT-CATCHER** *pulls* **PETE** *away. In a farewell gesture to the* **BAND,** **PETE** *hands his groovy sunglasses off to* **GRUMPY TOAD.***)*

PETE. Don't worry about me, fellas. They can't lock me up for good. Just you wait, I'll be out before you know it and we'll be jamming again!

START TRACK 01C

CAT-CATCHER.
LET'S FIND YOU A HOUSE.

PETE. *(Spoken in rhythm.)*
ON NO, NOT THAT!

CAT-CATCHER.
A LESSON IN MANNERS IS OVERDUE.

PETE.
BUT I AIN'T A HOUSECAT! NO SIREE.

CAT-CATCHER.
TOO BAD!
IT'S A FAM'LY FOR YOU.

PETE. *(Spoken in rhythm.)*
A FAM'LY?

CAT-CATCHER. *(Spoken in rhythm.)*
THE BIDDLES.

PETE.
WELL, IF IT'S A HOUSE I'VE GOTTA DO,
THAT'S AN ADVENTURE, TOO
I'M STILL PETE, YOU CAN'T MAKE A PET OUTTA ME.

PETE.	**CAT-CATCHER.**
LIFE IS A REALLY, REALLY,	OOH...
REALLY BIG ADVENTURE	
I NEVER TURN AWAY	OOH...
FROM AN ADVENTURE.	
AND EV'RYWHERE I GO IS	OOH...
AN ADVENTURE.	...VENTURE

> *(The* **CAT-CATCHER** *deposits* **PETE** *at the* **BIDDLES'** *house.)*

PETE. 1432 Maple Street. The Biddle Family.

(To audience.) Well, you know what I always say? Pete Philosophy:

> *(A musical fanfare accompanies his philosophy.)*

Life takes courage; be brave!

START TRACK 01D

> *(1432 Maple Street. On the other side of the door...)*

> *(***JIMMY*** *enters with a gigantic stack of books.)*

JIMMY. Yay! I'm studying! It's the last week of second grade and I have a lot of tests. The house is perfectly quiet and perfectly clean and perfectly perfect for... studying!!!

> *(The* **PARENTS** *enter, neurotically, trailed by Jimmy's little sister,* **OLIVE***, who is so excited.)*

DAD. Sandy, do we need more tuna?

MOM. Arthur, we have two hundred cans of tuna! Stop worrying.

OLIVE. Cat!

JIMMY. What's going on?!

OLIVE. We're getting a cat, we're getting a cat.

JIMMY. Today?

MOM. Yes, today.

JIMMY. But I –

DAD. I'm worried. I just don't know if we're cat people.

MOM. Stop worrying! Olive wants a pet, and a fish can't cuddle, so we're going to give this cat a try. I know we're all worried. Let's pretend we're cat-sitting for a friend.

OLIVE. Cat-sitting?

JIMMY. Mom, I'm worried.

MOM. Oh Jimmy,

> *(They squeeze together to make a perfect family portrait and look their very best for the guest.)*

MOM & DAD.
WHENEVER WE MEET SOMEBODY NEW,
IT'S NATURAL TO BE NERVOUS.
BUT NERVOUS PANIC IS HOW WE SHOW THAT WE CARE.

JIMMY, OLIVE, MOM & DAD (BIDDLES).
LIFE IS A REALLY, REALLY, REALLY BIG ADVENTURE.

JIMMY. I know.

BIDDLES.
A REALLY, REALLY, REALLY BIG ADVENTURE.

JIMMY. Fine.

BIDDLES.
A BIDDLE FAM'LY BEAUTIFUL ADVENTURE.

MOM.
GIVE THE CAT A CHANCE!

JIMMY.
I'LL GIVE THE CAT A CHANCE.

MOM & DAD.
LET'S ALL LOOK OUR BEST.

DAD.
AFTER ALL, HE IS OUR GUEST.

(They freeze with frozen grins.)

*(On the other side, **PETE** is at the door.)*

PETE. Well, here goes.

*(**PETE** knocks.)*

*(The **BIDDLES** move as a family clump to the door. It swings open. They are there, very square, grinning.)*

Hi.

BIDDLES. Who are you?

MOM. I'm sorry, we're expecting a cat.

JIMMY. We're cat-sitting.

OLIVE. We're gonna sit on a cat!

DAD. Go away.

(They slam the door.)

START TRACK 01E

JIMMY. *(Consulting book.)* Cat fact: cats do not wear shoes or say "hi." It says here, in my book.

*(The **BIDDLES** all ad-lib agreement.)*

DAD.	**MOM.**
That's right.	Well exactly, I've never –

*(**PETE** knocks again.)*

PETE. Hi again!

START TRACK 01F

YOU'RE EXPECTING A CAT; I THINK THAT'S ME.
ALL I NEED IS A COUCH ON WHICH TO CRASH.
I THINK IT'S AWFULLY GROOVY HERE, HELLO! HELLO?

OLIVE. Cats don't talk.

PETE.
MEOW?

MOM. Oh he is a cat! You must be Pete.

PETE.
MEOW, MEOW, MEOW!
THAT MEANS "HELLO" IN CAT.

DAD. Oh!

PETE.
MEOW, MEOW! MY NAME IS PETE!
I'M PLEASED TO MEET YA.
CAN YOU DIG IT?

DAD. Is that a guitar?

PETE. Sure is, take it away Dad!

*(***PETE*** gives ***DAD*** the guitar, and ***DAD*** rocks out.)*

BIDDLES.
MEOW, MEOW, MEOW, HELLO, HELLO!

DAD.
I'M ARTHUR.

MOM.
SANDY.

JIMMY.
JIMMY.

OLIVE.
AND OLIVE.

BIDDLES.
WE'RE PLEASED TO MEET YOU.

OLIVE.
AND WE CAN DIG IT!

PETE. Do you guys know how to jam? Olive?

> *(He offers his tail as a microphone.* **MOM** *and* **DAD** *giggle and dance.)*

MEOW!

OLIVE.

MEOW.

PETE. Sandy!

MOM & OLIVE.

MEOW.

PETE. Arthur!

MOM, DAD & OLIVE.

MEOW.

PETE. Jimmy!

ALL.

MEOW!

MOM, DAD & OLIVE.

I THINK THAT I LIKE HIM.
WHAT A CAT!
MAYBE WE ARE CAT PEOPLE.
SOMETHING ABOUT HIM JUST INSTANTLY PUTS ME AT
   EASE.

DAD. *(Spoken in rhythm.)*
WHAT DO YA KNOW?

MOM & OLIVE.	**PETE, JIMMY & DAD.**

LIFE IS A REALLY,
   REALLY, REALLY BIG
	LIFE IS A REALLY,
	   REALLY, REALLY BIG
	   ADVENTURE.

BA-NEO-NEOW!
A GROOVALICIOUS
   BEAUTIFUL
	A GROOVALICIOUS
	   BEAUTIFUL ADVENTURE.

ALL.

RELAX AND LET'S ALL HAVE A BIG ADVENTURE.

PETE.

  HELLO.

MOM.

  HERE'S A BOWL OF MILK.

  HERE'S SOME TUNA.

  HERE'S SOME TREATS
    FOR YOU.

JIMMY, DAD, & OLIVE.

  MEOW.

DAD.

  A SCRATCHING POST,

  A RUBBER MOUSE,

  A BALL OF STRING,

  SOME MITTENS!

PETE.

  MEOW.

JIMMY, MOM & OLIVE.

  HELLO.

OLIVE. *(Excited, spoken in rhythm.)*

  WHEN CAN I SIT ON HIM?

PETE. Yikes!

MOM & DAD.

  JUST IGNORE THAT.

BIDDLES.

  WE'RE SO PLEASED TO MEET YOU, PETE THE CAT!

(They riff a new family jam.)

PETE.

  BE NEO NA NA
    NEOW

  BA-NA-NEO-
    NA-NEOW!

JIMMY & DAD.

  PETE THE CAT.

OLIVE.

  BE NEO-NA-NA-
    NEOW

MOM.

  PETE THE CAT.

PETE.

  BLRNEOW-NEO-
    NEO-NEOW!

OLIVE.

  BA-NA-NEO-NA-
    NEOW!

MOM.

  PETE THE CAT

JIMMY.
> HE'S A CAT.   **OLIVE.**   **MOM & DAD.**
> A CAT. A CAT.   PETE-A-LEE   BE NEO-NA-NA-
PETE.   DETE-A-LEE   NEOW
> BLRNEOW-NEO-   DETE-A-LEE
> NEO-NEOW!   DETE-A-LEE
JIMMY.
> A CAT. A CAT.   PETE THE CAT!   BA-NA-PETE
>   THE CAT!

> *(They all embrace **PETE** in a clump, the song buttons, but then…)*

OLIVE. *(Sneeze!)*

BIDDLES. Uh oh.

MOM. Olive are you sneezing?

JIMMY. Cat fact: ten percent of the US population has cat allergies which make them sick.

PETE. Is Olive allergic to cats?

DAD. No.

OLIVE. *(Sneeze!)*

DAD. Yes.

MOM. *(Very embarrassed about the mistake.)* We have to send the cat back.

OLIVE. No!!!!!

JIMMY. Where does he go if we send him back?

MOM. The pound.

PETE. The pound…

MOM. Arthur, if she's allergic, we should really send him back.

DAD. Or…

ALL. Or...?

DAD. He can stay in...Jimmy's room!

JIMMY. *My* room?

DAD. Your room!

ALL BUT JIMMY. Yay!

JIMMY. Oh dear!

> *(The following lines may be said in transition if needed.)*

MOM. *(Exiting.)* Arthur you are really good on that guitar.

DAD. *(Exiting.)* Thank you, Sandy.

[MUSIC NO. 02 – LIFE IS AN ADVENTURE (PLAYOFF)]

START TRACK 02

(Transition to...)

Scene Two: Jimmy's Room

(Jimmy's room.)

JIMMY. Well here we are. My room is your room. Mi casa su casa. Meow is your ow, har dee har. *(Snort.)* It's probably not as nice as – where did you live before?

PETE. My Bus.

JIMMY. Your Bus?

PETE. Cool room. This rocket is so cool. Zoom.

JIMMY. Oh please be careful! That took me three whole months to make! Rockets go here. Your shoes can go there.

PETE. Cool. I see, you're, like, neat and clean.

JIMMY. *(Proudly.)* Yup.

PETE. Not me! I like to let it all hang out.

JIMMY. *(Consulting a book.)* But my book says cats are naturally tidy creatures.

PETE. That's housecats, but, see, I'm a *road cat. (He stretches.)* So Jimmy-oh, where can I jam?

JIMMY. Jam?

PETE. Make music?

> **(PETE** *"jams," which is an elaborate fun riff of air-drums, air-guitar, and other air-instruments.)*

(Air drumming, etc.) Buh buh buh bop bop bop bop neow buh buh bop ne-neow!

JIMMY. Not now. It's bedtime. Let me go get you a pillow.

> **(JIMMY** *exits.)*

PETE. Well look at me, Pete, in a bedroom, with a "bedtime," and a *bed*. Oh dude I wanna bounce on that bed so bad.

> (**OLIVE** *pokes her head in.*)

OLIVE. G'night Pete.

PETE. Oh, Olive!

OLIVE. Do you like my pyjamas, they have cookies. *(Sneeze.)*

PETE. Bless you, snazzaroo.

OLIVE. Hahaha. Pete, I didn't get to hug you before.

PETE. Pete Philosophy:

[MUSIC NO. 03 – PETE PHILOSOPHY]

START TRACK 03

> *(A musical fanfare accompanies his philosophy as they hug and she sneezes.)*

Ya gotta love a hug.

> (**JIMMY** *returns with a handwritten sign, shooing* **OLIVE**, *who dashes out.*)

JIMMY. Olive, out! You know the rules: No Girls Allowed.

PETE. The rules?

[MUSIC NO. 04 – HAPPY ROOMMATES]

START TRACK 04

JIMMY. Yes, they're pretty simple.
THESE ARE THE RULES OF MY ROOM:
NUMBER ONE IS THERE'S NO GIRLS ALLOWED.
NUMBER TWO IS THE ROCKET ALWAYS GOES ON THE SHELF.

So I need you to put that back.

JIMMY.

> FOOD'S NOT ALLOWED IN MY ROOM.
> SO NUMBER THREE IS YOU CANNOT HAVE FOOD.
> AND NUMBER FOUR IS YOU MAY NOT LEAVE UNDERWEAR
>   ON THE FLOOR.

> Of course, this is all perfectly obvious to you.
> AND ALSO PLEASE DON'T SHED,
> ESPECIALLY ON THE BED.
> AND WE'LL BE HAPPY, HAPPY ROOMMATES.
> HAPPY, HAPPY ROOMMATES.
> I GUESS I LIKE MY PRIVATE SPACE BUT ALSO I CAN SHARE.
> HAPPY, HAPPY ROOMMATES.
> HAPPY, HAPPY ROOMMATES.
> AND IF YOU CAN ONLY JUST STOP SHEDDING YOUR HAIR,
> WHAT HAPPY, HAPPY ROOMMATES WE'LL BE.

PETE. Great!

JIMMY. Good, now repeat them back to me.

PETE. Huh, oh!

> NUMBER ONE IS NO ONE'S ALLOWED, AND NUMBER TWO
>   IS THAT...

JIMMY. No girls. No Girls Allowed.

PETE.

> NUMBER

START TRACK 04A

> TWO IS THAT THINGS SHOULD BE CLEAN, AND NUMBER
>   THR–

JIMMY. No!

PETE. Things should be messy?

JIMMY. No! Things should be clean, but that's rule numbers fifteen through thirty-five, not number two. Oh dear.

PETE. *(Striking air guitar chord.)*
NUMBER

START TRACK 04B

THREE IS AT SEVEN, WE JAM!

(Maybe some drumming here.) Wink wink.

JIMMY. That's funny,
BUT

START TRACK 04C

JAMMING'S NOT ALLOWED IN MY ROOM.
YOU CAN JAM MAYBE IN THE GARAGE.
(THERE ARE NO RULES THERE.)
BUT RIGHT NOW, IT IS SEVEN, AND SEVEN IS TIME TO
    BRUSH TEETH.

PETE.
BRUSH TOES?

JIMMY.
NO I SAID BRUSH TEETH.

PETE. *(Spoken in rhythm.)*
TOES?

JIMMY.
BRUSH TEETH, TEETH, TEETH!

PETE.
TOES?

PETE & JIMMY.
HAPPY, HAPPY ROOMMATES.
BRUSHING TEETH TOGETHER.

JIMMY.
HERE'S AN EXTRA DISINFECTED TOOTHBRUSH FOR YOU.
HAPPY DISINFECTING.

PETE.
BRUSHY, BRUSHY, BRUSHY.

JIMMY.
> THIS IS JUST A LITTLE GLIMPSE OF ALL THE THINGS THAT WE TWO
> HAPPY, HAPPY ROOMMATES WILL DO.

PETE. *(Walking in circles on the bed, like cats do.)* Where am I gonna sleep? Here!

JIMMY. My bed?

> (**PETE** *flops down on Jimmy's bed.* **JIMMY** *gingerly climbs into a teeny tiny corner of the mattress.)*

PETE.
> HAPPY, HAPPY ROOMMATES.
> HAPPY, HAPPY ROOMMATES.
> COMFY?

JIMMY. *(Spoken in rhythm.)*
> UH HUH…

PETE.
> OKAY BUDDY, NIGHTY NIGHT!

PETE & JIMMY.
> HAPPY, HAPPY ROOMMATES.
> HAPPY, HAPPY ROOMMATES.

PETE.
> A FELLA COULDN'T ASK FOR A COZIER BED TO TUCK THESE
> HAPPY, HAPPY ROOMMATES IN TIGHT.

PETE & JIMMY.
> HAPPY, HAPPY ROOMMATES…

PETE.
> ALRIGHT.

JIMMY. Um. Pete? Thing is I really need to get some sleep tonight because tomorrow there's a really important *test* at *school,* and – Pete?

(**PETE**'s *asleep.*)

JIMMY. Oh.

So, great! Good talk.
GOODNIGHT.

Scene Three: School

[MUSIC NO. 05 – SCHOOL! (TRANSITION)]

START TRACK 05

(Alarm clock! **PETE** *and* **JIMMY** *get their things and rush to school as music underscores.)*

JIMMY. I'm late!!!!

(In the transition, **MRS. CREECH** *marches in with* **STUDENTS**, **ELOISE** *and* **BARNABY**, *a prim, proper, studious group, preparing for a test.)*

BARNABY & ELOISE.
SCHOOL. SCHOOL. SCHOOL.
SCHOOL. SCHOOL. SCHOOL.

MRS. CREECH. *(Operatically.)*
SCHOOL IS NICE AND SCHOOL IS FUN
SCHOOL IS GOOD FOR EV'RYONE.

BARNABY & ELOISE.
SCHOOL. SCHOOL. SCHOOL.
SCHOOL. SCHOOL. SCHOOL.

MRS. CREECH. Ah, class, today at school, we take our big test! And it's a math test!

*(***JIMMY** *and* **PETE** *enter on a skateboard.)*

Jimmy Biddle, you are late for class.

JIMMY. Sorry, Mrs. Creech! My parents had to take my sister to the doctor, so my cat had to walk me to school. This is my cat. Thanks Pete, Bye Pete.

MRS. CREECH. Pete the Cat? *The* Pete the Cat? *(Flustered.)* I just *love* your band.

PETE. Awesome.

MRS. CREECH. Would you stay for the test? We'd love if you would stay.

PETE. Cool!

JIMMY. Pete can't stay –

MRS. CREECH. Class, since Pete the Cat is here, maybe we shouldn't have a math test. Pete, what's your favorite subject?

PETE. I like art.

MRS. CREECH. Oh! Art!

(*Naughty:*) Let's have an art test!

PETE. Cool!

JIMMY. But Mrs. Creech! The art test is supposed to be on Friday!

ELOISE.	**BARNABY.**
Yeah.	I'm confused.

PETE. Chill out, Jimmy, I got this.

[MUSIC NO. 06 – PAINTING]

START TRACK 06

PUT DOWN YOUR PENCILS.
IT'S TIME FOR ART!
GO GET THE PAINT OUT
CUZ WE'RE GONNA START
PAINTIN'
RED AND BLUE AND YELLA,
WE'RE PAINTIN'.
YOU'RE A REAL ARTISTIC FELLA,
PAINTIN' WITH MY FRIENDS.
THE GOOD TIME NEVER ENDS.
OO OO OO
IT'S COOL TO PAINT AT SCHOOL.

MRS. CREECH. *(Fussy.)* It is cool! To paint at school!

> *(They've got their pads and easels now and nobody knows what to do.)*

JIMMY. But Mrs. Creech, no one's ready for an art test. What are we supposed to be painting?

MRS. CREECH. Anything!

KIDS. *(Amazed.)* Anything???!!

JIMMY. *(Upset.)* Anything?!

MRS. CREECH. *(Truly dismayed.)* Oh no. Pete! I don't have a paintbrush for you.

PETE.
> THAT'S NOT A PROBLEM.
> DON'T LOOK SO PALE.
> I MAY NOT HAVE A BRUSH
> BUT I DO HAVE A TAIL!
> I'M PAINTIN'.

ELOISE.
> HE'S PAINTIN' WITH HIS TAIL!

PETE.
> I'M PAINTIN'.

BARNABY. I wish *I* had a tail!

PETE.
> IF YOU DON'T HAVE A TAIL,
> YOU CAN USE YOUR FINGERNAIL.
> OO OO OO
> IT'S COOL TO PAINT AT SCHOOL.

ELOISE.	**BARNABY.**
Ha ha!	I'm using my elbow!

JIMMY. But we have brushes! I'm using my brush. This is *chaos.*

*(The **KIDS** get painting, all but **JIMMY**, who
is stuck, and doesn't know what colors to use.)*

ELOISE.

CAN I USE GREEN?

MRS. CREECH. Yeah!

BARNABY.

CAN I USE BLUE?

MRS. CREECH. Awesome!

JIMMY.

BUT MINE'S NOT PRETTY...

PETE.

IF IT'S PRETTY TO YOU,
THEN PAINT IT.

MRS. CREECH.

PAINT IT.

PETE.

PAINT IT.

MRS. CREECH.

PAINT IT.

PETE.

YEAH!

MRS. CREECH. *(Operatically.)*

YES!

*(Everyone's having a party. Except **JIMMY**,
who is stuck and panicking.)*

JIMMY.

I DON'T KNOW WHAT TO PAINT.
CUZ I DON'T KNOW WHAT'S BEST.
AND I THINK I MIGHT FAINT.
MRS. CREECH, MRS. CREECH, CAN I TAKE A DIFF'RENT TEST?

MRS. CREECH.
WHO KNEW THAT SCHOOL COULD BE COOL?

START TRACK 06A

ELOISE & BARNABY. *(Spoken in rhythm.)*
COOL! COOL! COOL!

ELOISE, BARNABY, PETE & MRS. CREECH.
WE'RE PAINTIN'

ELOISE.
ALIENS ON MARS!

ELOISE, BARNABY, PETE & MRS. CREECH.
WE'RE PAINTIN'

BARNABY.
DINOSAURS IN CARS.

PETE.
PAINT WHAT MAKES YOU GLAD.

PETE & MRS. CREECH.
PAINT WHAT MAKES YOU HAPPY OR SAD.

PETE.
OO OO OO.
THERE AIN'T NO PAINTIN' RULE.

MRS. CREECH.	**BARNABY & ELOISE.**
(Opera gliss.)	
AH!	OO OO OO.

PETE.
JUST BE A PAINTIN' FOOL.

MRS. CREECH.	**BARNABY & ELOISE.**
GETTIN' GROOVY WITH	OO OO OO.
YOU!	

PETE.
IT'S COOL TO PAINT AT SCHOOL.

(Everyone has gotten very concentrated as the test draws to a close. **JIMMY** *spies on* **ELOISE***'s painting.* **MRS. CREECH** *evaluates everyone's work.)*

MRS. CREECH. Please put your finishing touches on those masterpieces. Very nice, Eloise.

ELOISE. It's an alien warrior ninja monk from Mars.

MRS. CREECH. Well that's very special. And Jimmy?

JIMMY. It's an alien warrior ninja monk from Mars...

MRS. CREECH. You copied?

START TRACK 06B

ELOISE, BARNABY & PETE.
COPYING.
NOT COOL NOT COOL NOT COOL.

JIMMY. I know! I'm sorry, Mrs. Creech, I didn't mean to!

MRS. CREECH.
JIMMY BIDDLE,
YOU FAILED,
YOU COPIED,
YOU BLEW IT!
BY TOMORROW,
BRING ME AN ORIGINAL PAINTIN' THAT YOU HAVE MADE,
AND IF YOU CANNOT DO IT –

JIMMY. I don't know if I can do it.

MRS. CREECH.
– JIMMY BIDDLE, YOU WILL NEVER PASS THE SECOND GRADE!

ELOISE, BARNABY & PETE.
NOT COOL NOT COOL NOT COOL NOT COOL NOT COOL.

MRS. CREECH, ELOISE, BARNABY & PETE.
NOT COOL!

(**MRS. CREECH, ELOISE,** *and* **BARNABY** *march off.*)

(*Transition.*)

[MUSIC NO. 07 – AFTER SCHOOL/ FAMILY JAM]

START TRACK 07

(**PETE** *approaches* **JIMMY** *gingerly.*)

PETE. Whoa Jimmy.

JIMMY. *(Shell-shocked.)* I got in trouble.

> (**JIMMY** *starts walking.* **PETE** *has to scramble to keep up.*)

PETE. Jimmy, J-bug. That was crazy. I think we could both use some ice cream, don't you?

JIMMY. Why did you have to change it to an art test?

PETE. Sorry.

JIMMY. I didn't study for an art test! I studied for a *math* test.

PETE. You can just paint another painting.

JIMMY. I can't! I *copied* another kid, now I'm in trouble! Mom and Dad are gonna be so mad!

> (**JIMMY** *runs off.*)

PETE. Jimmy! *(To audience.)* I didn't mean to get him in trouble. Aw! This housecat stuff is tough, man.

> (**PETE** *chases after* **JIMMY.** *Transition to inside, where…*)

Scene Four: Home

START TRACK 07A

*(The **BIDDLES** are jamming! With swiffers and pots and pans. Square people trying to let loose. They ad-lib silly stuff about rocking out. "Groovy!" "Yeah!" etc.)*

MOM, DAD & OLIVE.
LIFE IS A REALLY, REALLY, REALLY BIG ADVENTURE.
WE'RE JAMMING AND IT'S SUCH A BIG ADVENTURE.
A MOM AND DAD AND OLIVE JAM ADVENTURE.

*(But as **JIMMY** and **PETE** try to sneak by behind them, **OLIVE** sneezes.)*

PETE. Bless you!

MOM. Oh Pete. Update: Olive is definitely allergic to cats.

DAD. She just needs an s-h-o-t.

OLIVE. No shots!!!!!

DAD. She's afraid of shots, but she is a very good speller.

OLIVE. Kitty, I love you, but I cannot get a shot.

PETE. I love you too, Olive.

OLIVE. Really?

(She gets an idea and runs off, squealing in delight on her exit.)

(Exiting, thrilled.) Eeeeeee meow!

MOM. Jimmy, how was test day?

JIMMY. Everything was great at school. Nothing's wrong!

START SFX TRACK 07B

(The phone rings.)

DAD. The phone!

JIMMY. What phone! I don't hear a phone?

MOM. Who could that be? *(To* **DAD**.*)* It's Mrs. Creech! Jimmy's teacher!

PETE. Oh no.

JIMMY. Mrs. Creech.

MOM. *(So upset.)* Oh no.

DAD. What?

MOM. She says Jimmy copied.

DAD. *(Alarmed.)* Jimmy did *what*?!

JIMMY. It's true! I'm never gonna graduate second grade! I'm going to go hide, and don't come looking for me!

　　　　(**JIMMY** *runs off.*)

MOM. *(Hanging up phone.) Jimmy Dean Biddle!!*

DAD. I can't believe he copied.

PETE. Whoa, Biddles, Jimmy needs our help right now.

DAD. He was always such a good kid!

MOM. This isn't like him at all!

PETE. Everyone's allowed to make a mistake. Right? Arthur? Sandy? We can't just let Jimmy hide all by himself. He needs us.

MOM. *(Softening.)* Oh Arthur, he's right.

PETE. Let's all go look for him. Where would a scared little kid go?

DAD. I'll look in his room!

　　　　(He exits.)

MOM. I'll look in the garage!

(She exits.)

PETE. I'll look –

*(**OLIVE** returns in a tutu with a wedding veil and bouquet.)*

OLIVE. Kitty. Kitty. Hey kitty.

PETE. Have you seen –

OLIVE. I love you. Can we get married?

[MUSIC NO. 08 – THE SNEEZING SONG]

START TRACK 08

(Music sting.)

PETE. What?

OLIVE. I love you and I wore my tutu.

START TRACK 08A

PETE. Whoa.

OLIVE. And you said you love me, so now nothing can keep us apart.

START TRACK 08B

Not even a stuffy nose!

PETE. *(Uh-oh.)* Whoa whoa, meowza wow!

OLIVE.

I'M ALLERGIC TO YOU.
IT'S A LITTLE BIT GROSS.
I'M ALLERGIC TO YOU,
SO IT'S HARD TO BE CLOSE.
IT'S MY MOST ANNOYING FLAW.
I LOVE EV'RY WHISKER, EV'RY CLAW.
CUZ I DON'T NEED TO BREATHE.
DON'T BE CRAZY, SAY YES.
WE'LL HAVE THE ROCKINGEST WEDDING
WE CAN BOTH WEAR A DRESS!

OLIVE.
AND INSTEAD OF SAYING VOWS,
WE'LL DO SNEEZES AND MEOWS!

(Spoken in rhythm.)
AH AH CHOO!
AH AH CHOO!

(Sung.)
I LOVE MY ALLERGIES, KITTY BE MY MAIN SQUEEZE.
I LOVE TO SNEEZE FOR YOU.

PETE. Gee, Olive, but I'm looking for Jimmy.

OLIVE. I have a tutu for you too, Pete!

(He runs, she chases, the way little kids do with cats.)

PETE.
THIS IS ALL VERY SWEET

OLIVE. Kitty kitty!

PETE.
BUT I'M FRANKLY UNSURE.

OLIVE. C'mon!

PETE.
DON'T YOU THINK YOU COULD BE HAPPY
WITH THE PUPPY NEXT DOOR?

OLIVE.
EV'RY NOSE TWITCH IS A SIGN.
WHEN I SNEEZE IT HAS TO MEAN "BE MINE!"

(Spoken in rhythm.)
AH AH CHOO!
AH AH CHOO!

(Sung.)

I LOVE MY ALLERGIES, IT'S LIKE A LOVE DISEASE.
I LOVE TO SNEEZE FOR YOU.

*(She tries to put the tutu on **PETE**.)*

PETE. Watch the tail!

OLIVE.

	PETE.
I'LL TAKE THE HEADACHES AND THE ITCHING	WHOA!
AND THE BRONCHIAL CONGESTION FOREVER,	WHOA!
	I'M NOT COOL WITH THAT!
AND EVER.	
	I'M NOT THAT KINDA CAT!
I DON'T MIND	OLIVE, NO
CUZ WHEN YOU FIND THE ONE,	NO!

OLIVE.

AND IT'S REAL, AND YOU KNOW...

PETE.

I DUNNO?!

OLIVE.

THEN YOU MUST NEVER, NEVER, NEVER,

PETE.

NEVER NEVER!

OLIVE.

NEVER LET THEM GO.

(She traps him.)

I'M ALLERGIC TO YOU.
AND I LIKE THAT, IT'S FUN!

OLIVE.
I'M LIKE SO OVERDOSED,
BUT MY NOSE CAN JUST RUN.
SO YOU DON'T NEED TO CHANGE A HAIR
CUZ MY SNEEZES SHOW HOW MUCH I CARE.

(Spoken in rhythm.)

AH AH CHOO!
OH YEAH!
AH AH CHOO!

*(All sly and cat-like, **PETE** dives behind the couch to hide. Oblivious, **OLIVE** continues rocking.)*

I LOVE MY ALLERGIES, YOU GOTTA MARRY ME, PLEASE.
YOU CAN HEAR ALL MY "I LOVE YOUS" IN EV'RY WHEEZE.
I LOVE TO SNEEZE FOR YOU.
FOR YOU, FOR YOU!

(Spoken in rhythm.)

AH CHOO!

*(But where is **PETE**?)*

Kitty kitty?

(She exits in search of him.)

[MUSIC NO. 09 – AFTER SNEEZING SONG]

START TRACK 09

*(**PETE**'s head emerges from behind the couch, amused.)*

[MUSIC NO. 10 – HAPPY HOUSECAT]

START TRACK 10

PETE.

THAT WAS KIND OF CRAZY.
ALSO KIND OF FUNNY.

They're nice.

EV'RYONE ON MAPLE STREET IS BONKERS TODAY!
THIS IS MY NEW FAM'LY.
THEY REALLY KIND OF LIKE ME,
SO HOW'M I GONNA TELL 'EM THAT I REALLY CAN'T STAY
SOME HAPPY, HAPPY HOUSECAT...
CUZ I AM NOT A HOUSECAT!
COULD I BE A HOUSECAT?

Whoa.

NO WAY!

But I still gotta find Jimmy...

[MUSIC NO. 11 – TO COUCH]

START TRACK 11

(*As* **PETE** *exits,* **JIMMY** *enters over transition music, on his way to his hiding place.*)

JIMMY. Everyone's so mad. To think, this morning I was still a perfect kid. But now? Now there's nowhere to go...but one place...

START TRACK 11A

Scene Five: Underneath the Couch

(Scene change! With a lift of the backdrop, in a blink, we're underneath the couch. **JIMMY** *sits, maybe a little proud of his secret spot.)*

JIMMY. Under The Couch. The perfect hiding place. I'll disappear like an old penny, a useless Cheeto, yeah, nobody will *ever* find me *here.*

(At that, **PETE** *slides in.)*

JIMMY & PETE. Whoa!
You!?
What are *you* doing here?

PETE. Jinx!

JIMMY. *(Grimacing.)* Rr!

PETE. Found ya. Hey Biddles I found Jimmy! He's under the co –

*(***JIMMY*** covers* **PETE***'s mouth.)*

JIMMY. Shush! Aaaaa Pete! I'm trying to *hide.* First you ruin test day and then you tattle-tale?

PETE. I didn't mean to mess up your day.

JIMMY. You had to pick art! I'm the *worst* at art!

(The parents pop their heads in.)

DAD. Oh there you are! Found him! Sandy! Jimmy's under the couch with Pete!

MOM. Under a couch? How crazy!

JIMMY. Mom.

DAD. It's really dusty down here!

MOM. I'm covered in dust!

DAD. Me too!

MOM. We're disgusting!

(*Pulling him out.*) Okay, Jimmy, let's go.

JIMMY. (*Digging in.*) No.

PETE. Come on, Jimmy.

JIMMY. No!

[MUSIC NO. 12 – UNDER THE COUCH]

START TRACK 12

(*May be rhythmically spoken, unpitched.*)

I'M NOT A CAT! I WILL NEVER BE COOL!
AND I CAN NEVER FACE THE PEOPLE AT SCHOOL!
I'M NOT A PAINTER! I'M FINISHED, I'M THROUGH!
(*Sung.*)
I DON'T KNOW WHAT TO DO!

PETE.
(*Spoken in rhythm.*)
YOU DON'T KNOW WHAT TO DO?
(*Sung.*)
WELL, YOU GOTTA GET OUT!

MOM, OLIVE & DAD.
OUT!

PETE.
MY FRIEND!

MOM, DAD & OLIVE.
FRIEND!

PETE.
GET OUT FROM UNDER THE COUCH!

MOM, DAD & OLIVE.
OUT FROM UNDER!

PETE.

IT'S NOT

MOM, DAD & OLIVE.

NOT!

PETE.

THE END!

MOM, DAD & OLIVE.

NO NO!

PETE.

GET OUT FROM UNDER THE COUCH!

MOM, DAD & OLIVE.

LET'S GET UP AND GO...

PETE.

THINGS ARE BLEAK, I KNOW IT'S TRUE
BUT FACE THE WORLD LIKE HEROES DO,
AND I BET YOU'LL FIND
YOU'VE GOT A PAINTIN' IN YOU.

(Everyone agrees.)

JIMMY. But aren't you mad at me for copying?

MOM & DAD. Oh Jimmy.

DAD.

WE LOVE YOU TO BITS.

MOM.

WE'RE REALLY NOT MAD.

DAD.

EVEN WHEN YOU MESS UP,

BOTH.

YOU'VE GOT MOM AND DAD!

MOM, DAD & PETE.

AND YOU GOTTA GET OUT!

JIMMY. *(Spoken in rhythm.)*
BUT –

MOM, DAD & PETE.
BE BRAVE!

(**OLIVE** *appears somewhere, maybe jumping up behind the couch backdrop.)*

OLIVE. *(Spoken in rhythm.)*
BE BRAVE!!!!

MOM, DAD & PETE.
GET OUT FROM UNDER THE COUCH.

JIMMY.
I'M NOT READY!

PETE.
ONE MISTAKE'S NOT GONNA BREAK YA.

JIMMY.
I *LIKE* IT UNDER THE COUCH!

MOM, DAD & OLIVE.
LET'S GET UP AND GO...

PETE.
LOOSEN UP, NOW DON'T BE SHY
AND I WILL BE YOUR BACK-UP GUY!
IT MIGHT JUST BE FUN
IF YOU CAN GIVE IT A TRY.

MOM, DAD & OLIVE.
GIVE IT A TRY!

JIMMY.	**MOM, DAD & OLIVE**.
MAYBE IF I HAVE SOME HELP.	OO...
MAYBE THINGS ARE NOT SO BAD.	
MAYBE IF I HAVE A FRIEND TO LEAD THE WAY ...	AH

PETE.
A FRIEND IS WHAT YOU FOUND TODAY.

(**PETE** *extends his hand.* **JIMMY** *takes it.*)

PETE. Give it to me Biddles!

ALL. Yeah!

(*Everyone cheers.*)

(**PETE** *and* **JIMMY** *begin to dance baby-steps toward leaving the couch.*)

PETE.
STICK YOUR TOE OUT FROM UNDER THE COUCH.
STICK YOUR TOE OUT FROM UNDER THE COUCH.
(*Spoken in rhythm.*)
ONE TOE.

PETE & JIMMY.
GET YOUR FOOT OUT FROM UNDER THE COUCH.
GET YOUR FOOT OUT FROM UNDER THE COUCH.

PETE & JIMMY.	**MOM, DAD & OLIVE.**
AND YA INCH OUT	GET OUT, GET OUT.
FROM UNDER THE COUCH	GET OUT, GET OUT.
YEAH, YA INCH OUT	GET OUT, GET OUT,
FROM UNDER THE COUCH	GET OUT.

JIMMY. So dusty!

PETE & JIMMY.	**MOM, DAD & OLIVE.**
AND YA ZIG ZAG	GET OUT, GET OUT.
ON OUTTA THE COUCH	GET OUT, GET OUT.
YEAH, YA ZIG ZAG	GET OUT, GET OUT,
ON OUTTA THE COUCH.	GET OUT.

JIMMY. The crumbs!

PETE & JIMMY.	**MOM & OLIVE.**	**DAD.**
AND WE'RE HIP WIGGLIN'	GET OUT, GET OUT.	OO…
OUTTA THE COUCH.	GET OUT, GET OUT.	
WE'RE A-HIP WIGGLIN'	GET OUT, GET OUT,	
OUTTA THE COUCH.	GET OUT.	
		GET OUT!
THEN WE'RE ROCK ROLLIN'	GET OUT, GET OUT.	OO…
OUTTA THE COUCH.	GET OUT, GET OUT.	
WE'RE A-ROCK ROLLIN'	GET OUT, GET OUT,	
ALL THE WAY OUT.	GET OUT.	

JIMMY.
LET'S GO!

PETE.
LET'S GO!

JIMMY.
LET'S GO!

BIDDLES.
LET'S GO!

PETE. *(Shouted in rhythm.)*
OW!!

ALL.
GET OUT!
LET'S MOVE!
GET OUT FROM UNDER THE COUCH.

PETE.

YEAH!

BIDDLES.

GO ON!

LET'S GROOVE.

OUT FROM UNDER THE
COUCH!

PETE.

GROOVE.

PETE.

AND IT DON'T FEEL SO BAD. AREN'T YOU GLAD TO BE
OUT FROM UNDER, THOUGH IT WAS COZY?

PETE.

WE ALL FALL DOWN,

BIDDLES.

AH

PETE.

YEAH, WE ALL FALL DOWN,
BUT WE GET BACK UP, CUZ A WISE GUY KNOWS 'EE
CAN'T STAY UNDER THE COUCH.

MOM, DAD & OLIVE.

NO, NO, NO!

PETE & JIMMY.

HE CAN'T STAY UNDER THE COUCH.

MOM, DAD & OLIVE.

OUT FROM UNDER THE COUCH,
YOU GOTTA GET OUT FROM UNDER THE COUCH

JIMMY & PETE.

UNDER THE COUCH.

MOM, DAD & OLIVE.

GET OUT FROM UNDER THE COUCH, YOU GOTTA

ALL.

GET OUT FROM UNDER THE COUCH!

*(They dance their way out, returning to the
real world...)*

Scene Six: Inspiration

DAD. Okay, Jimmy, we love you.

MOM. We love you. Good luck!

OLIVE. Kitty kitty –

> (**MOM** *and* **DAD** *drag* **OLIVE** *away.*)

DAD. No, Olive, leave kitty alone!

> (*The* **BIDDLES** *exit.*)

JIMMY. *(Getting pumped:)* I'm pumped! I'm pumped! Hwuh! I got my hips wigglin'!

PETE. Yeah!

JIMMY. *(Loose.)* I got my zig zaggin'!

PETE. Yeah!

JIMMY. *(Almost there.)* Now I just gotta get my brush brushin' and –

PETE. Paintbrush!

> (**PETE** *hands him the brush and he immediately freezes.*)

JIMMY. Oh *no.*

It's the paintbrush! I wanna paint the *best* painting but I freeze, I just freeze.

PETE. Whoa! It's just a painting.

JIMMY. It's not! It has to be the *best*, most *beautiful* painting of the *best*, most *beautiful* thing.

PETE. Then we better go see a bunch of beautiful things so you can find the best one. And I know just the way. Jimmy-o, we shall go *(Momentously:)* in the *Veee W Bus.*

[MUSIC NO. 13 – BUS REVEAL]

START TRACK 13

(Musical flourish as **PETE** *summons the Bus onto the stage.)*

PETE. Hello Bus!

START SFX TRACK 13A

(The Bus honks hello. Hello!)

JIMMY. The what?

PETE. VW Bus! The V is for Very, the W is for Wonderful. It's a very wonderful bus.

JIMMY. Are you sure it's safe?

PETE. *(Covering Bus's ears.)* Hey! Be nice. The Bus is sensitive.

START SFX TRACK 13B

(The Bus honks unhappily: "Not nice. ☹")

This beautiful Bus is gonna take us to the best, most beautiful sights so *you* can paint the best, most beautiful painting, okay? *But* the Bus won't start until you say something kind.

JIMMY. Sorry. *(To Bus.)* Bus, you're a Very Wonderful Bus, Bus.

[MUSIC NO. 14 – IT'S A VW BUS]

START SFX TRACK 14

(The boys lurch as the Bus roars up! Happy honk: "Let's get going!")

PETE. Atta Bus!

JIMMY. Wow!

PETE.

> JIMMY COME AND LEMME SHOW YA
> ALL THE PLACES WE CAN GO
> IN THE BIG V DOUBLE-U BUS.

JIMMY. Yeah!

PETE.

> WHEN YOUR BRAIN IS SUPER FRIED,
> THEN YOU MIGHT JUST NEED A RIDE
> IN A HIP V DOUBLE-U BUS.

> *(Bus honk: "Ain't this fun?")*

> IT MAY LOOK LIKE A WRECK
> BUT IT JUST NEEDS A KICK
> AND IT GOES ROUND THE WORLD!

JIMMY. *(Spoken in rhythm.)*
CAN IT GET US THERE QUICK?

PETE.	**JIMMY.**
VRUM-VRUM-VRUM VRUM-VRUM, A V DOUBLE-U BUS.	WHOOOOOAAA

PETE & JIMMY.

> V DOUBLE-YA BUS!
> V DOUBLE-YA BUS!
> V DOUBLE-YA BUS!

PETE.

> IT'S A V DOUBLE-YA BUS!

> *(Unseen by **JIMMY** and **PETE**, a **SHARK** fin has floated through above them. They land at the bottom of the ocean.)*

JIMMY. Holy snorkels, are we underwater?

PETE. It's the bottom of the ocean! Excellent idea, Bus.

  *(The **SHARK** swims into the scene.)*

JIMMY. *(Panicked.)* Shark!

PETE. It's cool, he's friendly.

SHARK. Yo.

PETE. See?

JIMMY. It's a friendly ocean. Yeah! There's stuff here I can paint.

SHARK. Oh, you are a painter? Well why don't you paint me? I am a very good model. *(Posing.)* Pose, pose, pose.

JIMMY. I'm not really a *painter*. I'm just doing homework.

SHARK. Well, you better not make my nose look big.

JIMMY. Huh?

SHARK. I suppose if you do, I'll probably have to eat you.

JIMMY. Eat me??!

  *(The **SHARK** laughs. Urgent Bus honk: "Let's get out of here!")*

PETE. Bus says we gotta go!

JIMMY. Thank you Bus!

  *(The Bus takes off again, riding the wave to the next stop. Perhaps the **SHARK** continues trying to model as they go.)*

PETE.
 BETTER BUCKLE IN TIGHT.

JIMMY.
 BETTER PULL UP MY SOCKS.

JIMMY & PETE.
 CUZ THE ONLY WAY TO ROLL'S
 WITH AN ENGINE THAT ROCKS!
 VRUM-VRUM-VRUM VRUM-VRUM, A V DOUBLE-U BUS.

ALL.
V DOUBLE-YA BUS!
V DOUBLE-YA BUS!
V DOUBLE-YA BUS!

PETE & JIMMY.
IN A V DOUBLE-YA BUS!

(They land on the moon, and **JIMMY** *and* **PETE** *start bouncing a little.)*

JIMMY. Where are we now? Why am I bouncing?

PETE. It's the moon, Jimmy!

(An **ASTRONAUT** *bounces through.)*

ASTRONAUT. No gravity on the moon!

*(***JIMMY** *laughs, bouncing.)*

PETE. Yo astronaut, what's the most beautiful thing you've ever seen?

ASTRONAUT. Why, I like to look at the Earth out there in the distance and marvel at how tiny it is.

JIMMY. *(Writing in notepad.)* "Look – at – tiny Earth."

PETE. *(Tipping* **JIMMY**'s *face up.)* No, Jimmy, *look* at tiny Earth.

JIMMY. Oh. It's beautiful.

PETE. Yeah.

JIMMY. *(Almost sold.)* I could paint that.

But remember Pete, it has to be the *best, most beautiful* painting. I just don't know if this would be it. Bus? Um. I wonder if you have any more ideas?

(Bus honks: "I got a million ideas.")

Where next?

PETE. Let's find out.

JIMMY & PETE.
AND WHEREVER WE GO,
WE ALL GOTTA SMILE.
YEAH, THE DECADES CAN CHANGE,
BUT WHAT'S ALWAYS IN STYLE,
VRUM-VRUM-VRUM VRUM-VRUM, A V DOUBLE-U BUS.

ALL.
V DOUBLE-YA BUS!
V DOUBLE-YA BUS!
V DOUBLE-YA BUS!

PETE. Yeah, the Renaissance. Hey Jimmy, that's the *Mona Lisa*. It's a very famous painting.

JIMMY. A real expert!

PETE. Hi Mona.

MONA LISA. *(Trashy accent.)* Heyyyy.

JIMMY. What a pretty painting.

MONA LISA. Thanks, doll.

JIMMY. *(Enjoying it.)* The eyes. The hair. It's beautiful. It's perfect. *(Heart-crashing.)* Oh no, it's perfect!! Pete! Someone already painted the best, most beautiful painting.

>   *(The Bus issues warning alerts. Not honks, but rather, some dire, negative alarms.)*

PETE. Jimmy!

JIMMY. I can't do anything like that! Not even close! I'm just a kid. No one can help me. Not even the stupid Bus!

>   *(Suddenly, like it's breaking down, honk, the Bus returns home, where **OLIVE** is in her pj's, brushing her teeth.)*

PETE & JIMMY. Whoa. Home?

OLIVE. Hi guys.

PETE. The Bus brought us home because you said it was stupid.

JIMMY. Oh Bus, I didn't mean it! I'm just upset. Bus, I'm sorry.

OLIVE. Why is there a Bus in the bathroom?

PETE. Jimmy. You don't need to paint the *Mona Lisa*. You just gotta paint what you think is beautiful.

JIMMY. Well I don't know what that is! And the painting's due tomorrow morning. It's already bedtime. We should just give up.

START SFX TRACK 14A

(Sheepish honk: "Um, guys?")

PETE. What's that, Bus? *(Goes to Bus, listening, we get one half of the conversation.)* Mm hmm. Uh huh. What do you think? I'll tell him.

JIMMY & OLIVE. What did it say?

START SFX TRACK 14B

PETE.
WHEN YOU'RE ALL OUT OF HOPE
AND THE SKY'S LOOKIN' GRAY,
YOU'RE AT THE END OF YOUR ROPE,
YOU NEED TO SEE A NEW WAY... YOU NEED...
THE MAGIC SUNGLASSES.

JIMMY & OLIVE.
THE MAGIC SUNGLASSES.

PETE. But! They're in France.

JIMMY & OLIVE. France??

PETE. At the Jam Café, in Paris France, on my buddy Grumpy Toad's face.

JIMMY. Let's go!

PETE. Let's go! (*As* **OLIVE** *follows.*) Not you, Olive.

OLIVE. Yes me, or I'll tell Mom you went to Paris after bedtime.

JIMMY & PETE. Fine.

PETE. Give the Bus some love!

OLIVE. (*To Bus.*)
BUS, YOU'RE
VERY WONDERFUL.

JIMMY.
VERY WONDERFUL.

JIMMY & OLIVE.

INCREDIBLY WONDERFUL,	**PETE.**
AMAZINGLY WONDERFUL,	TO THE
WONDERFUL.	JAM CAFÉ TO FIND A
	NEW WAY TO SEE,
WONDERFUL.	GONNA GET THOSE
	GLASSES,
	GOTTA GO TO PAREE!

JIMMY.	**OLIVE.**	**PETE.**
Woah!	Wow!	Yeah!

(*Happiest of honks! Let's get going!* **MONA LISA** *tags along.*)

ALL.
WE'RE A-WHIRRIN' AND A PURRIN',
INSPIRATION IS A-STIRRIN'.

MONA LISA.
OH, I LOVE A V DOUBLE-U BUS.

(**MONA LISA** *claps her hands.*)

JIMMY.

COME ON, FLOOR IT!

ALL.

IT'S A HUNKY BUNCHA JUNK
WITH A MERMAID ON THE TRUNK.

MONA LISA.

SO UNIQUE, V DOUBLE-U BUS.

JIMMY.

HURRY, HURRY!

*(MONA LISA
claps her hands.)*

PETE.

IT'S THE SHAPE OF A BEETLE,
BUT DON'T CALL IT A BUG.
WHEN THE ENGINE GETS TO SQUEALIN',
SHE ONLY WANTS A HUG.

(He floors it and the Bus takes off, losing
MONA LISA. *Our travelers wave goodbye.)*

JIMMY.

TO THE JAM CAFÉ!

PETE & OLIVE.

VROOM!

JIMMY.

TO FIND A NEW WAY TO SEE ...

PETE & OLIVE.

VROOM!

*(There's a crazy vocal breakdown as they
journey on.)*

JIMMY.

WE ARE OFF TO
PAREE!

OLIVE.

TO PAREE!

PETE.

TO PAREE!

PETE, JIMMY & OLIVE.
>IN A V DOUBLE-YA BUS.
>V DOUBLE-YA BUS!
>V DOUBLE-YA BUS!
>V DOUBLE-YA BUS!

JIMMY.	**OLIVE.**	**PETE.**
IN A V DOUBLE-YA HOO	IN A V DOUBLE-YA BUS.	IN A V DOUBLE-YA BUS.
V DOUBLE-YA YEAH,	PETE! PETE!	DUB DUB DUB DUB DUB
V DOUBLE-YA OO,	I'M TALKIN' 'BOUT PETE!	DUB DUB DUB DUB DUB
V DOUBLE-YA OW!	PETE! PETE! I'M TALKIN' 'BOUT PETE!	DUB DUB DUB DUB DUB!
IN A V DOUBLE-YA BUS.	IN A V DOUBLE-YA BUS.	IN A V DOUBLE-YA BUS.
WHAT A BUS	V-V-V-V-V-V HOO!	WHAT A BUS
WHAT A BUS	V-V-V-V-V-V YEAH! WAH WAH WAH WAH WAH	WHAT A BUS
OH YEAH BUS!	WAH OH!	OH YEAH BUS!

JIMMY.
>IN A V DOUBLE-U –

OLIVE.
>IN A V DOUBLE-U –

PETE.
>IN A V DOUBLE-U –

OLIVE, PETE & JIMMY.
>BUS!

>*(They roar off to...)*

Scene Seven: Paris!

[MUSIC NO. 15 – PARIS MAGIC]

START SFX TRACK 15

(Magical Paris music under the transition. Actors ad-lib as they change the scenery, a silly arrival in Paris.)

PETE, JIMMY & OLIVE. Paris! Awwwwww.

(If needed:) Baguettes! The Eiffel Tower! City of Lights! France!

(When the door is set…)

PETE. The Jam Café!

JIMMY. I need the magic sunglasses!

PETE. C'mon. There's a secret knock.

(He does the secret knock. A hand emerges from the door with a note.)

OLIVE. A note!

JIMMY. Is that normal?

PETE. Uh, no. Let's see, it says: "No kids allowed."

JIMMY. Oh no.

OLIVE. Do we have to go home? Hey! You in there! Look at me, I'm hip to the beat!

(She does a dorky move and sneezes.)

Ahchoo! Ahchoo! Blech.

PETE. Oh gosh, I didn't think of this. I'm not sure how to get you guys in.

JIMMY. What's your plan, Pete?

PETE. I, I, I don't have a plan.

JIMMY. I do!!! Ta da! I packed us disguises!

PETE. Disguises?

OLIVE. Disguises! Yay Jimmy!

> (**JIMMY** *pulls some silly disguises out of his suitcase.*)

JIMMY. I like to plan for all occasions. Here we go. Olive, you put on this mustache.

OLIVE. Oh, yes, that's very French.

JIMMY. And I have fancy French hats and scarves. Ta-da!

PETE. Jimmy, you're amazing.

JIMMY. Do we look French? And grown-up?

PETE. Totally French. And *so* grown-up.

OLIVE. Hahaha, so grown-up!

JIMMY. Jimmy Biddle Philosophy:

[MUSIC NO. 16 – JIMMY PHILOSOPHY]

START SFX TRACK 16

(Nerdy musical fanfare.)

Be Prepared.

PETE. Okay, your name is Pierre LeSneeze! Well, here goes nuthin'.

[MUSIC NO. 17 - JAM JAM (TRANSITION 1)]

START SFX TRACK 17

GUS THE PLATYPUS & GRUMPY TOAD.
JAM JAM! *(Clap Clap.)*
JAM JAM! *(Clap Clap.)*
JAM JAM! *(Clap Clap.)*
JAM JAM! *(Clap Clap.)*

PETE. Voila: The Jam Café.

There's Gus the Platypus, there's Grumpy Toad on keytar. And there's...

OLIVE & JIMMY.
THE MAGIC SUNGLASSES!

JIMMY. That's them, isn't it? Those sunglasses will definitely help me paint my painting. Pete how do I get them?

PETE. Yo band!

GUS THE PLATYPUS. Pete the Cat?!!!

PETE. Gus! Grumpy Toad!

GRUMPY TOAD. Yo Pete!

GUS THE PLATYPUS. Pete's back in the band!

[MUSIC NO. 18 - JAM JAM (TRANSITION 2)]

START SFX TRACK 18

PETE, GUS THE PLATYPUS & GRUMPY.
JAM JAM! *(Clap Clap.)*
JAM JAM! *(Clap Clap.)*

OLIVE. *(Too enthusiastically.)* JAM JAM!

(Music out.)

PETE. Guys, actually, I want to introduce you to my pal Pierre. Say hi Pierre.

JIMMY. *(So squarely.)* Jam jam, um, hi.

PETE. Grumpy Toad, Pierre needs to borrow those sunglasses, the magic sunglasses.

GRUMPY TOAD. These magic sunglasses?

JIMMY. Yeah! I need them to help me –

GRUMPY TOAD. *(Taking them off.)* Whaddya want with these old things?

JIMMY. Cuz they're magic.

PETE. *(Taking sunglasses.)* Yeah.

> *(**PETE** puts on the glasses.)*

[MUSIC NO. 19 – MAGIC WORLD]

START SFX TRACK 19

> *(Magic music plays as he looks at the world.)*

Ooo.

JIMMY. What?

PETE. Whoa.

JIMMY. What?

PETE. Yeeeeah.

JIMMY. Pete!

PETE.
> OH, WHAT A VIEW.
> I WISH YOU COULD SEE.
> SUDDENLY EV'RYTHING'S BEAUTIFUL TO ME.
> IT'S LIKE WHOA, OH MAN, IT'S A MAGIC WORLD.
> WHOA, OH MAN, IT'S A MAGIC WORLD.

JIMMY. *(Reaching.)* That's what I need.

GRUMPY TOAD. Me too, give 'em back!

GUS THE PLATYPUS. No, I want 'em!

> *(**GUS THE PLATYPUS** gets 'em. Magic music as he looks at the groovy world.)*

PETE. What do ya see Gus?

GUS THE PLATYPUS. Very groovy. So many colors.

JIMMY. Argh!

GUS THE PLATYPUS.
OH, WHAT A VIEW.
IT'S JUST LIKE A DREAM.
EV'RYTHING'S PRETTY AS PEACHES AND CREAM.
IT'S LIKE WHOA, OH MAN, IT'S A MAGIC WORLD.
WHOA, OH MAN, IT'S A MAGIC WORLD.

(*He hands 'em to* **GRUMPY TOAD.** *They pass them back and forth.*)

GRUMPY TOAD.
WHOA, OH MAN, I MEAN WHOA, OH MAN

JIMMY. (*Shouted in rhythm.*)
HEY!

GUS THE PLATYPUS.
WHOA, OH MAN, I MEAN WHOA, OH MAN –

JIMMY. (*Shouted in rhythm.*)
HEY!

GRUMPY TOAD. Hey Pierre, how bad do you want these sunglasses?

JIMMY. Really really bad!

GRUMPY TOAD. Well, then prove it!
CAN YOU HOP ON ONE FOOT?

JIMMY.
I CAN HOP ON ONE FOOT.

GUS THE PLATYPUS. Nice!

GRUMPY TOAD.
CAN YOU SPIN LIKE A TOP?

JIMMY.
I CAN SPIN LIKE A TOP.

GRUMPY TOAD.
CAN YOU QUACK LIKE A DUCK?

JIMMY.

QUACK QUACK QUACK QUACK QUACK QUACK.

GRUMPY TOAD.

CAN YOU JAM LIKE A PRO?

JIMMY. *(Spoken in rhythm.)*
UM, THAT I DON'T KNOW…

Pete?

PETE. You have to! Keep going!
YOU CAN BOP BOP BOP SH-BOP BA-BOP BOP.

JIMMY.

I CAN BOP BOP BOP SH-BOP BA-BOP BOP.

PETE.

YOU CAN BIDDILY BOP BOP BOP SH-BOP BOP.

JIMMY.

I CAN BIDDILY BOP BOP BOP SH-BOP BOP.

PETE.

YOU CAN DOODLY DOOT.

JIMMY.

I CAN DOODLY DOT.

PETE.

YOU CAN BOODILY BOP.

JIMMY.

I CAN BOODILY BOP.

PETE.

BOP SH-BOW!

JIMMY.

BOP SH-BOW!

PETE.

BOW!

JIMMY.

BOW!

PETE.

NEOW!

JIMMY.

NEOW!

> *(Then!* **JIMMY** *jams like* **PETE** *jammed back in his bedroom, doing crazy air guitar, air drums, an air trumpet, like a whole silly one-man band, ending with air cymbals on someone's head – "pshhh!" – And a great big grin and sigh from having let loose.)*

> *(The* **BAND** *applauds, approving.)*

GRUMPY TOAD. Young sir. You have earned the Magic Sunglasses.

START TRACK 19A

> *(***GRUMPY TOAD** *and* **GUS THE PLATYPUS** *bestow the sunglasses upon* **JIMMY.***)*

ALL *(Except* **JIMMY***).*

THE MAGIC SUNGLASSES.
THE MAGIC SUNGLASSES.
THE MAGIC SUNGLASSES.

> *(***PETE** *brings the canvas and the paintbrush, and* **JIMMY** *begins painting. Note: the canvas should face upstage so the audience cannot see what* **JIMMY** *is painting. That's for later.)*

JIMMY.

I SEE MY PAINTING, I'M SEEING IT ALL IN A FLASH.
I'M PAINTIN' OLIVE DANCIN' IN HER MUSTACHE.
AND I'M FEELIN',
WOW! I'M FEELIN' FREE.

JIMMY.
> I'M PAINTIN' PETE AND THE WAY HIS FUR JUST SHINES.
> AND I'M EVEN COLORIN' OUTSIDE THE LINES
> CUZ I'M PAINTIN' EV'RYTHING I SEE.

PETE.
> YEAH, YOU ARE.

> (*As* **JIMMY** *rapturously paints,* **PETE** *removes the sunglasses from his face.*)

JIMMY. Hey, I need those!

PETE. No you don't.

Guess what. Those sunglasses aren't even magic.

JIMMY. But look, I'm painting.

PETE. Yeah! All by yourself! Who needs sunglasses!

> (**JIMMY** *looks at the room, his friends, and realizes he still feels cool and groovy.*)

JIMMY. Whoa!
> HEY, LOOK AT THAT!
> YOU'RE TOTALLY RIGHT.
> HEY AND IT'S STILL SUCH A BEAUTIFUL SIGHT.
> OH WHAT A VIEW.
> I TOTALLY SEE.
> SUDDENLY EV'RYTHING'S BEAUTIFUL TO ME!
> WHOA, OH MAN, IT'S A MAGIC WORLD.
> LET ME PAINT THIS MAGIC WORLD.

GRUMPY TOAD & GUS THE PLATYPUS. (*Shouted in rhythm.*)
> 1-2-3-4!

> (**JIMMY** *dives back into painting as the* **BAND** *jams around him.*)

OLIVE, GUS THE PLATYPUS & GRUMPY TOAD.
> JAM! JAM!

JIMMY.

I'M PAINTIN'!

OLIVE, GUS THE PLATYPUS & GRUMPY TOAD.

JAM! JAM!

PETE.

YOU'RE PAINTIN'.

OLIVE, GUS THE PLATYPUS & GRUMPY TOAD.

JAM! JAM!

JIMMY.	**OLIVE, GUS & GRUMPY.**
I'M PAINTIN' YOU, AND I'M PAINTIN' THE TOAD!	JAM! JAM!
I'M PAINTIN' WHAT WE SAW ON THE ROAD.	JAM! JAM!
I'M PAINTIN' THE BUS FLYIN' THROUGH THE DARK!	JAM! JAM!
I'M PAINTIN' THE MOON 'N' I'M PAINTIN' THE SHARK.	JAM! JAM!
IT'S NOT THE MOST BEAUTIFUL,	AHH...
IT'S SURE NOT THE BEST,	
BUT I'M GLAD I CAME TO PARIS,	
GONNA PASS THE TEST. AND IT'S	

ALL.

WHOA, OH MAN,
IT'S A MAGIC WORLD.

JIMMY & PETE.

WHOA, OH MAN, IT'S A MAGIC WORLD.

OLIVE, GUS THE PLATYPUS & GRUMPY TOAD.

OH, IT'S A MAGIC WORLD.

ALL.

YEAH!

(He puts the last brush strokes on the painting as the jam ends.)

(The song buttons. The room erupts into applause. **JIMMY** *takes confident bows.* **OLIVE** *dashes off. Separately,* **GUS THE PLATYPUS** *and* **GRUMPY TOAD** *exit.)*

JIMMY. Thank you, thank you.

PETE. Jimmy, you did it! Jimmy Biddle painted a painting!

JIMMY. Is it okay?

PETE. I love it.

(They admire the painting, though it is still hidden from the audience, facing upstage.)

JIMMY. Oh! Mrs. Creech! We gotta get to school. Where's the Bus, where's Olive – (*Realizing she's missing.*) Hey! Where's Olive?

PETE. (*Freaking.*) Whaddyamean, where's Olive?

*(***PETE*** *freaks out.* **GUS THE PLATYPUS** *returns and observes cool* **PETE** *freaking out.)*

Olive??

GUS THE PLATYPUS. Who's Olive?

PETE. She's just a kid! A kid.

JIMMY. She's only five.

GUS THE PLATYPUS. Pete the Cat is losing his cool.

JIMMY. It's my sister.

GUS THE PLATYPUS. Your sister? Pete the Cat is losing his cool over a little girl?

PETE. So what if I am? You know what? I love that little girl!

*(***OLIVE*** *saunters in, carrying tutus.)*

OLIVE. Well I have our wedding dresses. Do you know Paris has the *best* tutus!

PETE. Aw Olive!

    (**PETE** *wraps* **OLIVE** *up in a hug. She beams.* **JIMMY** *joins in.*)

JIMMY. Aw Olive! Never go away!

OLIVE. *(Sweetly.)*	**JIMMY.** *(Sweetly.)*
Aw, ow.	Rrr, Cat fur.

JIMMY. Aaaaah I'm gonna be late for school. We gotta go, we gotta go!

[MUSIC NO. 20 – A CAT NAMED PETE]

START TRACK 20

    (**JIMMY** *goes for the Bus.*)

PETE. Pronto!

    (*But* **OLIVE** *won't go until...*)

OLIVE. Pete, put on your tutu.

PETE. Aw man. *(He does it.)* Only for you, Olive.

    (**PETE** *does a twirl in his tutu.*)

OLIVE. Very pretty kitty.

GUS THE PLATYPUS. Whoa.

JIMMY. Total housecat.

    (**PETE** *and* **OLIVE** *hurry arm-in-arm to a silly wedding theme us they all get the Bus going.*)

PETE. Graduation awaits!

JIMMY. Off to school!

GUS THE PLATYPUS. G'bye! G'bye!

    (*Transition to...*)

Scene Eight: Second Grade Art Class

MRS. CREECH. Hello, hello, my dear second graders. But where is Jimmy Biddle?

> (**JIMMY** *runs in with* **PETE,** *still in his tutu, out of breath.* **JIMMY** *is a total mess, and loving it.)*

JIMMY. Wait! Mrs. Creech! I've got the painting!

MRS. CREECH. Jimmy!

JIMMY. It took me all night! But I did it!

MRS. CREECH. What did you paint?

JIMMY. This.

> (*At last,* **JIMMY** *reveals the painting, a clumsy but affectionate kid-drawn portrait of* **PETE** *surrounded by symbols of their adventures.)*

START TRACK 20A

IT'S A CAT NAMED PETE.
HE'S GOT BIG ROUND EYES.
HE'S DONE A WHOLE LOT OF STUFF
FOR A CAT OF HIS SIZE.
AND HE HOGS THE BED,
AND HE'S NOT REAL NEAT.
THAT'S MY PAL,
THE CAT NAMED PETE.

MRS. CREECH. Why Jimmy, this is the most beautiful, best painting.

JIMMY. Is it?

MRS. CREECH. Oh yes.

JIMMY. Why?

MRS. CREECH. Because you painted something you love.

PETE. A plus?

MRS. CREECH. A plus, plus...plus!

>*(She exits. **OLIVE** runs in, revealing a bandage on her arm.)*

OLIVE. Guys! Guys! I got the shot. So now I won't sneeze! We can have a slumber party in Jimmy's room.

PETE. Well Olive, rule number one is no girls allowed.

>*(**PETE** turns to **JIMMY**.)*

JIMMY. New rule! Olive's allowed!

>*(**OLIVE** snuggles in, brother-sister hug. Over top of her head, **JIMMY** speaks to **PETE**.)*

Jimmy philosophy: ya gotta love a hug!

PETE. Pete philosophy: How cool is it to be a housecat? Pretty cool.

>*(The whole **FAMILY** barges in.)*

BIDDLES.
HE'S A CAT NAMED PETE.
HE WEARS BRIGHT RED SHOES.
AND HE SURE STANDS OUT
IN THOSE GROOVY BLUES.
AND YOU'LL HEAR HIM COMING
WHEN HE ROLLS DOWN THE STREET
ON HIS YELLOW SKATEBOARD,
THE CAT NAMED PETE.

PETE.
THE SUN IS UP AND SHININ'.
THE BIRDS ARE SINGIN' AND THE SKY IS BRIGHT.
AND I'M FEELIN',
AND I'M FEELIN', I'M FEELIN',
AND I'M, I'M FEELIN'
ALL RIGHT!

BIDDLES.
> OH, HE'S A REAL COOL CAT
> AND HE CAN DRIVE A CAR.
> AND WHEN HE NEEDS TO THINK,
> HE LIKES TO PLAY THE GUITAR.
> HE LIKES HIS MUSIC COOL,
> AND HIS COFFEE SWEET!

OLIVE, MOM & DAD.
> HIS MUSIC COOL,
> AND HIS COFFEE SWEET!

JIMMY.
> AND HE'S MY BEST FRIEND,
> THE CAT NAMED PETE.

PETE.
> GROOVY!

BIDDLES.
> CAT NAMED PETE.

PETE.
> SO SWEET!

ALL.
> CAT NAMED PETE!

The End

[MUSIC NO. 21 – BOWS (VW BUS)]

START TRACK 21

*(After the bows, the actors reprise the end of
VW Bus. Honk honk honk!)*

ALL.

IT'S THE SHAPE OF A BEETLE,
BUT DON'T CALL IT A BUG.
WHEN THE ENGINE GETS TO SQUEALIN'
SHE ONLY WANTS A HUG!
VRUM-VRUM-VRUM VRUM-VRUM
A V DOUBLE-U BUS.

V DOUBLE-YA BUS!
V DOUBLE-YA BUS!
V DOUBLE-YA BUS!

*(The following all overlap, with **MOM** and
DAD joining in.)*

PETE.	**OLIVE & MOM.**	**JIMMY & DAD.**
IN A V DOUBLE-YA HOO	IN A V DOUBLE-YA BUS.	IN A V DOUBLE-YA BUS.
V DOUBLE-YA YEAH,	PETE! PETE!	DUB DUB DUB DUB DUB
V DOUBLE-YA OO,	I'M TALKIN' 'BOUT PETE!	DUB DUB DUB DUB DUB
V DOUBLE-YA OW!	PETE! PETE! I'M TALKIN' 'BOUT PETE!	DUB DUB DUB DUB DUB!
IN A V DOUBLE-YA BUS.	IN A V DOUBLE-YA BUS.	IN A V DOUBLE-YA BUS.
WHAT A BUS.	V-V-V-V-V-V HOO!	WHAT A BUS.
WHAT A BUS.	V-V-V-V-V-V YEAH!	WHAT A BUS.

OLIVE & MOM.
WAH WAH WAH
WAH WAH
PETE.   WAH OH!   **JIMMY & DAD.**
OH YEAH BUS!   OH YEAH BUS!

JIMMY.
IN A V DOUBLE-U –

OLIVE.
IN A V DOUBLE-U –

PETE.
IN A V DOUBLE-U –

(To audience.) What??

*(The **AUDIENCE** probably yells back, "Bus!")*

ALL.
BUS!

START TRACK 21A

(The actors wave goodbye and drive the Bus off.)

[MUSIC NO. 22 – EXIT MUSIC]

START TRACK 22